We hope you enjoy this book.
Please return or renew it by the due date.
You can renew it at **www.norfolk.gov.uk/libraries**
or by using our free library app. Otherwise you can
phone **0344 800 8020** - please have your library
card and pin ready.
You can sign up for email reminders too.

NORFOLK COUNTY COUNCIL
LIBRARY AND INFORMATION SERVICE

D0540196

First published in hardback in Great Britain by HarperCollins Publishers Ltd in 1987
First published in paperback by Collins Picture Lions in 2001
Revised paperback editions published by HarperCollins Children's Books in 2009 and 2014
This edition published by HarperCollins Children's Books in 2019

1 3 5 7 9 10 8 6 4 2

ISBN: 978-0-00-832603-6

Collins Picture Lions is an imprint of HarperCollins Children's Books.
HarperCollins Children's Books is a division of HarperCollins Publishers Ltd.

Text copyright © Michael Bond 1987
Illustrations copyright © R. W. Alley 1999
Front cover and final page illustrations copyright © R. W. Alley 2019

Visit our website at: www.harpercollins.co.uk

Printed and bound in China

MIX
Paper from
responsible sources
FSC® C007454
www.fsc.org

FSC is a non-profit international organisation established to promote the
responsible management of the world's forests. Products carrying the FSC
label are independently certified to assure consumers that they come
from forests that are managed to meet the social, economic and
ecological needs of present and future generations.

Find out more about HarperCollins and the environment at
www.harpercollins.co.uk/green

Michael Bond
Paddington
and the
Marmalade
Maze

Illustrated by R. W. Alley

HarperCollins *Children's Books*

One day, Paddington's friend, Mr Gruber, took him on an outing to a place called Hampton Court Palace.

"I think you will enjoy it, Mr Brown," he said as they drew near. "It's very old and it has over one thousand rooms. Lots of Kings and Queens have lived here."

Paddington always enjoyed his outings with Mr Gruber and he couldn't wait to see inside the Palace.

As they made their way through an arch, Mr Gruber pointed to a large clock.

"That's a very special clock," he said. "It not only shows the time, it tells you what month it is."

"Perhaps we should hurry, Mr Gruber," said Paddington anxiously. "It's half past June already."

They hadn't been inside the Palace very long before they came across a room which had the biggest bed Paddington had ever seen.

"Queen Anne used to sleep in it," said Mr Gruber.

"I expect they put the rope round it to stop her falling out when she had visitors," said Paddington, looking at all the people.

"This is known as the 'Haunted Gallery'," said Mr Gruber.
"They do say that when Catherine Howard's ghost passes
by you can feel a cold draught."

Paddington shivered. "I hope she's got a duffle coat like
mine!" he said.

Mr Gruber took Paddington to see the kitchen next.

"In the old days they used wood fires," he explained. "That's why there is such a high ceiling. There was a lot of smoke."

"I was hoping they might have left some Royal buns behind," said Paddington, licking his lips.

"Talking of buns," said Mr Gruber, "I think it's time we had our lunch."

He led the way outside and they sat down together on the edge of a pool.

As Paddington opened his suitcase he accidentally dropped one of his sandwiches into the water. It was soon alive with goldfish.

"They must like marmalade," said Mr Gruber. "I wonder if that's how they got their name?"

When they had finished their sandwiches, Mr Gruber took Paddington to see 'The Great Vine'.

"It's very famous," he said. "Every year they pick over five hundred bunches of grapes. Imagine that, Mr Brown!"

"I'm trying to, Mr Gruber," said Paddington. "I think I might plant a grape pip when I get back home."

Mr Gruber chuckled. "I'm afraid you will have a long wait, Mr Brown," he said. "That vine is over two hundred years old."

"Now," said Mr Gruber, "before we leave we must visit the famous maze. Sometimes it takes people hours to find their way out."

"I hope that doesn't happen to us," said Paddington. "My paws are getting tired."

"Perhaps it's time I took you home," said Mr Gruber.

Much to his surprise, the words were no sooner out of his mouth than everyone around them began to talk.

"Hey, that sounds a great idea," said a man in a striped shirt.

"Please to wait while I buy a new film for my camera," said a Japanese lady.

"I've never been inside a real English home before," said another lady. "I wonder if they serve tea?"

"Oh, dear!" whispered Mr Gruber. "They must think I'm one of the guides. What shall we do?"

"Mrs Bird won't be very pleased if they all follow us home," exclaimed Paddington. "She only has a small teapot."

Then he had an idea.

"Follow me," he called. "I think perhaps we ought to go in the maze after all."

"Are you sure we are doing the right thing?" gasped Mr Gruber, as he hurried on behind.

"Bears are good at mazes," said Paddington. "You need to be in Darkest Peru. The forests are very thick."

And sure enough, before Mr Gruber had time to say any more, Paddington led the way out, leaving everyone else inside.

"How ever did you manage to do that, Mr Brown?" gasped
Mr Gruber.

"Quickest visit I've ever seen," agreed the man in the ticket office.

"I used marmalade chunks to show where we had been," said
Paddington. "It's something my Aunt Lucy taught me before she
went into the Home for Retired Bears."

"But I thought you had eaten all your sandwiches," said Mr Gruber.

"I always keep a spare one under my hat in case I have an emergency," said Paddington. "That's something else Aunt Lucy taught me. She'll be very pleased when she hears."

And he stopped at a kiosk to buy a picture postcard so that he could write and tell her all about his day out.

That night when he went to bed, as well as the postcard and a pen, Paddington took some rope.

   "It's something Queen Anne used to do," he announced. "I've a lot to tell Aunt Lucy and I don't want to fall out of bed before I've finished."

Collect more fantastic books about

Paddington

Michael Bond
Paddington
The original story of the bear
from Darkest Peru
Illustrated by R. W. Alley

Michael Bond
Paddington
at St Paul's
Illustrated by
R. W. Alley
A brand new Paddington adventure

Michael Bond
Paddington
at the Zoo
Illustrated by R. W. Alley

Michael Bond
Paddington
the Artist
Illustrated by
R. W. Alley

Michael Bond
Paddington
at the Palace
Illustrated by
R. W. Alley

Paddington
at the Tower
Michael Bond
Illustrated by
R. W. Alley

Please look
after this
Bear! Thank
You.

More than 35 million Paddington books sold worldwide!